Gwen & Charmcaster

Editorial Director: Marge Kennedy
Retold by Janice Markham
Based on Episode #29 "A Change of Face" by Thomas Pugsley and Greg Klein

Grandpa Max and Gwen stood on the street in Salem, Massachusetts, right outside Ye Olde Costume Shoppe. Each of them wore old-fashioned outfits like the Puritans had worn back in the 1690s. They were waiting for Ben, Gwen's ten-year-old cousin, to step outside.

"Enough of this, Ben," Grandpa Max said, tapping on the door. "It's time to get out here."

"I feel like a dweeb," Ben said as he slowly stepped into the daylight, wearing knickers, a vest, and white stockings.

"That's because you *are* a dweeb," Gwen laughed.

"That's it! I'm changing!" Ben said, heading back into the shop.

"Oh, no, you're not," Grandpa Max said, grabbing Ben by the collar of his starched white shirt. "While visiting this city, which is full of history, there's nothing wrong with getting into the spirit of things."

Before they could continue the argument, they heard a loud explosion as a nearby building burst into flames. People ran quickly from the fire, scattering in every direction.

Grandpa looked at Ben and said, "You can go ahead and change now!"

"Yes!" Ben shouted, adding, "Goodbye, Zero; hello, Hero!" as he pressed down on his Omnitrix and turned into Stinkfly.

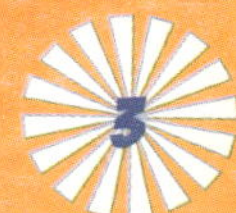

Standing amid the flames was the sorceress Charmcaster.

"*HAAAA!*" she cried out as she threw more fireballs at the street towards the fleeing people.

Ben, as Stinkfly, planned to sneak up on Charmcaster, but she was secretly watching him, hoping to draw him closer.

"That's it! Come into my parlour, said the spider to the Stinkfly," she laughed. She then shot a large purple sphere in Ben's direction, chanting, "*Transfera identica! Transfera identica! Transfera identica!*"

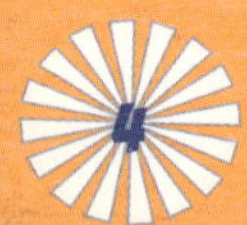

Gwen, meanwhile, had taken the reins of a runaway horse. She was bouncing along the cobble-stoned street when the horse made a sudden turn that sent her flying into the air—right into the bright purple light.

Charmcaster's plan was ruined! She had not switched bodies with Ben as she had intended. Instead, Charmcaster became Gwen, and Gwen became Charmcaster!

Stinkfly fell to the ground, feeling dazed.

He looked up and saw who he thought to be Gwen standing in front of him. But it was really Charmcaster, who now looked and sounded just like his cousin.

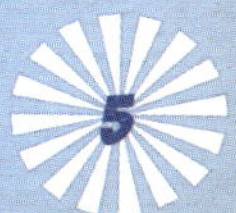

Stinkfly transformed back into Ben, and, with Grandpa Max, ran over to the Gwen look-alike.

"Are you okay?" Ben asked, helping Gwen to her feet.

"Yeah, sure, I'm fine," the imposter said, sounding just like Gwen. "It must have been Charmcaster causing all the trouble."

The real Gwen, looking like Charmcaster, watched the scene in horror.

"Ben! Grandpa!" she called out. But they couldn't hear her over the wail of fire engines. The fake Gwen hurried along the street, following Ben and Grandpa Max as they walked back to the Rustbucket, Grandpa's trusty Recreational Vehicle (RV).

A short time later, police officers spotted Gwen on the street. She matched the description of the fire starter. They quickly arrested her.

"Your new Home, Sweet Home is going to be the Juvenile Jail," they said as they put handcuffs on her wrists.

"I'm innocent! You've got the wrong person!" Gwen, looking and sounding like Charmcaster, pleaded.

"That's what they all say," the prison guard replied as she slammed the door shut.

Two somewhat scary teens approached Gwen, who, in her Charmcaster's costume, looked regal.

"Hi, Princess. I'm Pinky, and this is Missy," Pinky said. "And since you're new around here, I'll fill you in on the two rules you'll need to know. Rule One: What I say goes. Rule Two: Obey rule number one, or else!"

Ben was trying to forget his embarrassment about wearing the dorky Puritan costume earlier in the day as he stood outside the Rustbucket. He was soon interrupted by a familiar voice.

"So..." Charmcaster said, trying to act as Gwen would act. "Once you've dialled in the alien you want on your Omnitrix, you just slam it back down, and then you're ready to go on the attack?"

"Yeah, but you already know that," Ben said, looking a bit confused. "Hey, what gives? Since when are *you* interested in *my* hero mode? I thought you were only interested in magic and spells and junk like that."

Charmcaster shrugged.

"I think I've learned all I'm going to about that stuff. Right now, I'm just interested in what you can do."

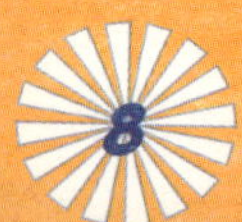

Ben raised an eyebrow and frowned.

"No, that's not it. You're setting me up to be punked somehow. Well, forget it. I'm too smart for you, Freak."

Ben started to walk away, but Charmcaster pushed him, and he landed on the ground. The Gwen look-alike then jumped down beside him and twisted his ankle, shouting, "Nobody calls me a freak and gets away with it! Nobody!"

Ben struggled to get away from her, screaming, "What's wrong with you?!"

Grandpa heard the disturbance and climbed down from the RV.

"What on earth is going on out here?" he demanded.

Ben pointed at the ten-year-old girl looming over him, still unaware of her actual identity. "Gwen snapped her cap. *That's* what's wrong," he said.

"Uh, Ben's right," the girl confessed. "It was all my fault, Grandpa. I started it. I'm sorry, Ben. Can you forgive me?"

"*Uh*, did you hit your head or something?" Ben asked, looking at her in confusion. Ben was used to Gwen picking on him. But apologising? That was new!

Back in the jail cafeteria, the real Gwen, looking like Charmcaster, sat at a lunch bench, staring at her tray of inedible food. As she rested her arm on the table, she felt something hard in the wide, flowing sleeve of her gown. Trying not to draw attention to herself, she quietly slid the object into her lap.

It was Charmcaster's book of magic spells! Gwen quickly scanned the contents and came across the heading "Body Transference Spells."

"So that's how she did it!" Gwen thought. But she couldn't understand why Charmcaster would want to change places with her. Then it hit her: "She wanted to switch places with Ben, not me! She's trying to get her hands on the Omnitrix."

Gwen then reached into the other sleeve of Charmcaster's gown and found a bag of magic eggs.

"*Hmm,*" she thought as she placed the eggs carefully back in the hidden pockets. "I may need these later."

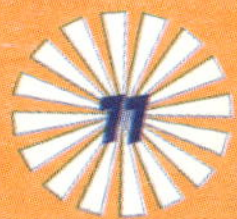

“Yo, Princess,” Missy said when she saw that Gwen was trying to hide something. “Whatcha got there? Have you been holding out on us?”

Gwen looked at Missy and Pinky, at the other girls slumped over their trays of awful food, and at Mrs Crabtree, the facility’s disgusting food server. She had an idea.

“*Food fight!*” she yelled, hopping up and tossing a spoonful of glob into the air.

Food flew in every direction. Everyone was either throwing food or getting hit by it. The melee distracted Missy from her interest in the book of spells. It also caught Mrs Crabtree’s attention.

“Hello! This is the cafeteria! I need Security now!” the woman screamed into the phone as Gwen intoned a spell from Charmcaster’s book *Bellum Hokoro Mazzura.*

Suddenly, Mrs Crabtree's ladle bent and wrapped around her arm. All the forks and spoons began marching towards her, ready to attack. A fearful Mrs Crabtree fell backward into a giant can of—well, no one could be sure. It could have been a can of beans or some other slop that passed for food in the jail. As Mrs Crabtree went *SPLAT*, the girls all cheered and clapped.

"Cool," Pinky said, looking in Gwen's direction. Gwen, as Charmcaster, bowed deeply to her audience.

Mrs Crabtree shook her fist in the air.

"You'll be scrubbing pots and pans until those pretty little hands fall off!" she said to Gwen, Pinky, and Missy.

While the real Gwen was locked away, Charmcaster convinced Grandpa Max and Ben to go with her to the Bait, Tackle & Fish store, where she planned to buy ingredients for a special feast.

"You guys wait here!" she said as they drove up to the front of the shop. As she closed the door of the Rustbucket behind her, she said to Ben, "I can't wait to cook for you tonight!" Then she went inside.

Ben smirked and whispered to Grandpa Max, "Uh, have you noticed that Gwen's been acting kind of weird today? I mean, weirder than normal."

"Just because she wants to follow in her grandfather's culinary footsteps doesn't mean she's weird, Ben," Grandpa said.

A few minutes later, Charmcaster emerged, holding a plastic container.

"Got it! The final ingredient," she declared triumphantly.

Grandpa Max opened the container and peered inside.

"Sea-urchin eggs?" he said. "Wow, those must've been expensive."

"Not really," the girl replied. "I sweet-talked them into giving me a deal."

What Ben and Grandpa didn't know was that the fake Gwen had used her Charmcaster strength to tie up the shop employees before helping herself to whatever she wanted.

Back at the Juvenile Jail, the real Gwen Tennyson, along with Missy and Pinky, was on clean-up duty as punishment for the food fight.

"I have to figure out how to get out of here!" she thought.

Mrs Crabtree stepped into the room to check on the girls, making sure they weren't planning any more surprises. She noticed the girl in Charmcaster's gown staring at her.

"What are you looking at?" Mrs Crabtree asked. "Just keep on mopping! And when you finish here, somebody gets to buff my bunions."

Mrs Crabtree walked away as Pinky started laughing, "Scrubbing the floor is a small price to pay for seeing the look on old Crabtree's face when she fell into that can of crud," she said. Then Pinky patted Gwen's shoulder. "You're all right, Princess," she whispered. Then she added, "Look if you ever need anything, just ask me."

"Actually, I need to find a way out of here," Gwen said.

Missy shook her head sadly.

"Armed guards are at every exit. There's no way you could ever..."

Just then, Gwen noticed a large, covered drain in the floor.

"Hey! I think I've found a way out, but we'll need a distraction," she said to her cohorts.

"No problem," Pinky replied.

With Missy's help, Pinky sprayed the guards with a blast of cold water. The guards slipped on the water and fell to the floor.

"Okay! This is my chance to get out of here!" Gwen said to herself. She pulled out a magic egg from Charmcaster's sleeve and tossed it in the direction of the still-sliding guards. The egg exploded, producing a smoke screen that provided the girls with all the cover they needed. They removed the drain cover and jumped down into the maze of pipes below.

The girls continued splashing through the drain system, searching for a way out. Soon they came to an area that looked out over the town, but it was blocked by sturdy bars.

"Man! Now what are we going to do?" an exasperated Missy said. "It's like we're locked up all over again!"

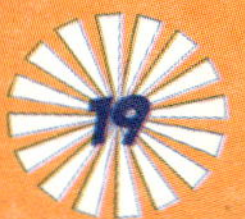

Gwen pulled another magic egg from her sleeve.

"Step back," she warned her companions. Before tossing it towards the bars, she turned to Pinky and Missy and asked, "If we get out of here, are you two going to change your ways and give up crime?"

"Not a chance!" Pinky answered. "We gotta make up for lost time. In fact, I feel a crime spree coming on!" Missy nodded her head in agreement.

Gwen decided that she needed to complete the escape on her own. She tossed the magic egg at the bars. Two strange animals suddenly appeared. Gwen squeezed her way past them and through the narrow opening in the bars that the animals had made. But the animals stood guard over the other girls and wouldn't let them pass.

As Gwen made her way out, the guards caught up with Missy and Pinky and dragged them back to the jail.

"If I ever see you again," Pinky screamed at Gwen, "you'll be sorry!"

It was evening in the harbour when Gwen found Ben outside the RV.

Ben looked at his cousin and hollered, "Charmcaster! Now I can lock you away myself!" He lunged towards her.

To buy herself some time, Gwen threw two magic eggs in front of him. The eggs turned into wild beasts, which growled and then knocked Ben over.

"Ben, I can't let you lock me up. Listen! The Gwen in the Rustbucket is not Gwen. I am! That's Charmcaster, who made herself look just like me. She did some kind of Transference Spell, and we wound up switching bodies."

"Don't believe her," Charmcaster shouted from the top of the stairs.

"All right, if you're really Gwen," Gwen shouted at Charmcaster, "then you should know the name of the teddy bear Ben sleeps with."

Ben folded his arms in embarrassment.

"Furry Freddy has his own bed. It just happens to be next to mine," Ben explained.

"You just gave her the answer, Dweeb!" Gwen said in exasperation. "Did your parents send you to doofus school, or were you born like this?!"

"Gwen!" Ben exclaimed when he heard the familiar insults. "It really is you!"

Gwen glared at Charmcaster and chanted, *"Transfera identica! Transfera identica! Transfera identica!"*

"NO! You can't use my spells on me!" Charmcaster yelled as Gwen's spell transformed both of them back into themselves. Charmcaster immediately searched her sleeves for her magic eggs and her book of spells, but they were gone.

"What did you do with my things?" she cried.

"Oh, sorry, they fell into the river," Gwen replied. "Now it's time to call the authorities!"

"Already done!" Grandpa Max declared. Within a minute, police arrived and tossed Charmcaster into their patrol car. The officers then brought Charmcaster back to jail, where Pinky and Missy were waiting for her.

Finally, back in the Rustbucket, Ben and Gwen argued about who should have to clean-up the cooking mess that Charmcaster had made. And they were both secretly happy to have everything back to normal.